# Snug as a Bug

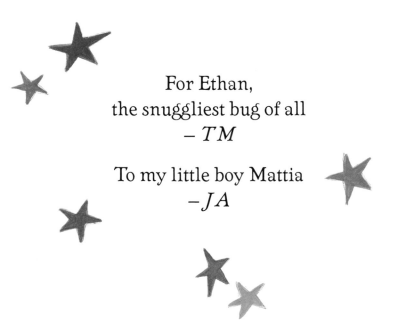

For Ethan,
the snuggliest bug of all
— *TM*

To my little boy Mattia
— *JA*

**Sandy Creek**
NEW YORK

An Imprint of Sterling Publishing
387 Park Avenue South
New York, NY 10016

This 2013 edition published exclusively for Sandy Creek by Simon & Schuster, London

ISBN 978-1-4351-4731-7

Manufactured in China
Lot #:
2 4 6 8 10 9 7 5 3 1
03/13

# Snug as a Bug

Tamsyn Murray & Judi Abbot

Sandy Creek
NEW YORK

The morning was gray,
   it was gloomy and dark,
when George and his mom
   got dressed for the park.

George folded his arms
    and started complaining,
"It's nasty and cold,
    and – look! – now it's raining!"

Mom gave a big smile.
"There may be some puddles,
so just to be safe
I've packed extra cuddles."

"You'll be as snug as a bug
rolled up in a rug,

like **two** cozy bats
in thick woolly hats.

As hot as **three** pigs
in big purple wigs,

wrapped up like **four** llamas in stripy pajamas.

As warm as **five** gnus in green furry shoes,

or **six** sizzling goats in red overcoats.

Like **seven** great apes
in long velvet capes,

or **eight** fish with flippers
in leopard spot slippers.

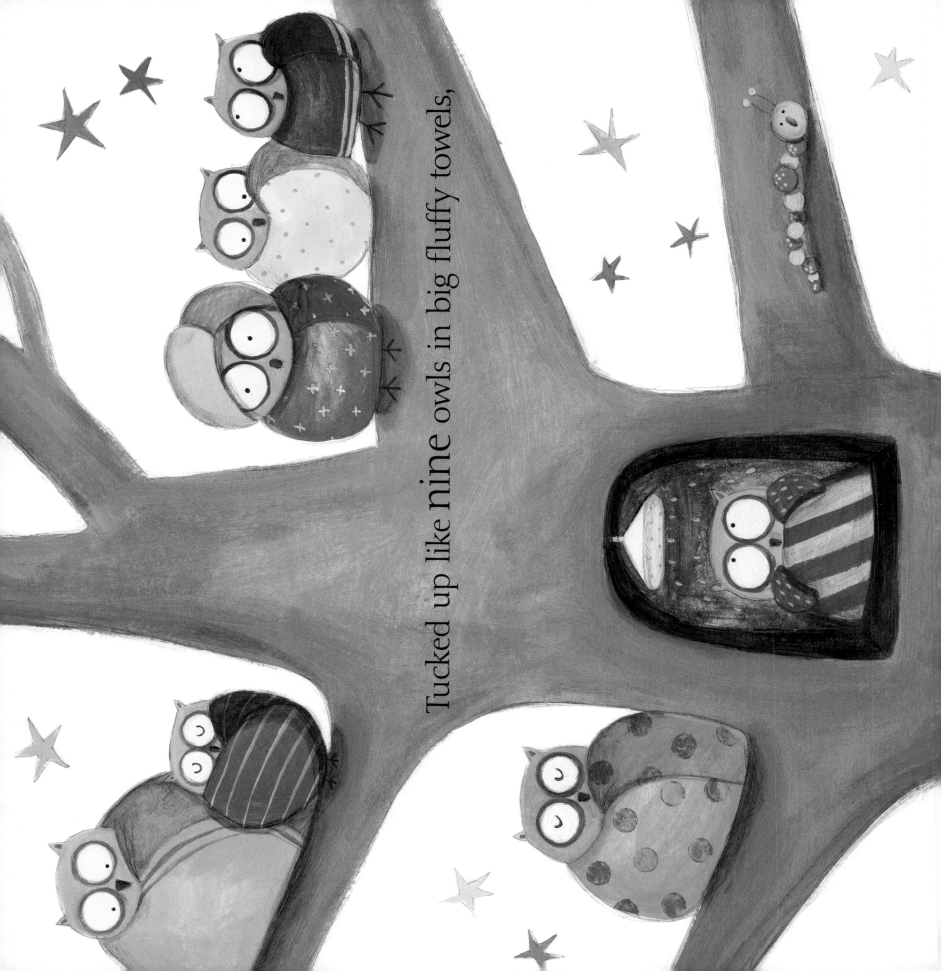

Tucked up like nine owls in big fluffy towels,

or ten toasty geese all sharing one fleece."

The park was such fun,
   it made George decide
to take off his coat
   as he went down the slide!

"Oh no," said his mom.
"Without that you might
get goosebumps or chills
or even frostbite!"

"You'll be like ten sneezy kittens without any mittens,

or **nine** frozen frogs
in huge wooden clogs.

As cold as **eight** bees
on miniature skis,

like **seven** long snakes
with icy milkshakes.

As chilled as **six** snails
caught out in strong gales,

or **five** fancy ants
in bright sparkly pants.

Like four polar bears
with tears in their flares,

as cool as **three** mice in skates on the ice.

Like **two** tall giraffes
with snowflakes for scarves,

or **one** freezy fox
with holes in his socks."

George thought very hard,
  he rubbed at his nose.
"Mommy, I'm cold
    from my head to my toes!"

Mom pulled on his coat.
   Her eyes shone with twinkles.
"So now's not the time
   for ice cream with sprinkles?"

Tucked up that evening, George gave Mom a hug.

"I think I prefer being . . .

snug as a bug!"